Michael Hague's
ILLUSTRATED

The Teddy Bears' Picnic

by Jimmy Kennedy

Henry Holt and Company ❖ New York

To Kasha—M.H.

Henry Holt and Company, Inc.
Publishers since 1866
115 West 18th Street
New York, New York 10011

Henry Holt is a registered trademark of Henry Holt and Company, Inc.

Text copyright ™ and © Warner/Chappell, Inc.
Used by permission.
Illustrations copyright © 1992 by Michael Hague
All rights reserved.
Published in Canada by Fitzhenry & Whiteside Ltd.,
195 Allstate Parkway, Markham, Ontario L3R 4T8.

Library of Congress Cataloging-in-Publication Data
Kennedy, Jimmy
The teddy bears' picnic/Jimmy Kennedy; illustrated by Michael Hague
Summary: A newly illustrated version of the song about teddy bears
picnicking independently of their "owners."
1. Children's songs—Texts, [1. Teddy bears—Songs and music.
2. Picnicking—Songs and music. 3. Songs.] I. Hague, Michael, ill. II. Title
[PZ8.3.K383Te 1992]
782.42164'0268-dc20   91-27709

ISBN 0-8050-1008-4 (hardcover)
3 5 7 9 10 8 6 4 2
ISBN 0-8050-5349-2 (paperback)
5 7 9 10 8 6 4

First published in hardcover in 1992 by Henry Holt and Company, Inc.
First Owlet paperback edition, 1997

Printed in the United States of America
on acid-free paper.∞

The
Teddy Bears' Picnic

If you go down in the woods today
You're sure of a big surprise.

If you go down in the woods today
You'd better go in disguise;

For ev'ry Bear that ever there was
Will gather there for certain, because
Today's the day the Teddy Bears
Have their picnic.

Ev'ry Teddy Bear who's been good
Is sure of a treat today.

There's lots of marvelous
Things to eat,
And wonderful games to play.

Beneath the trees where nobody sees
They'll hide and seek as long
As they please,

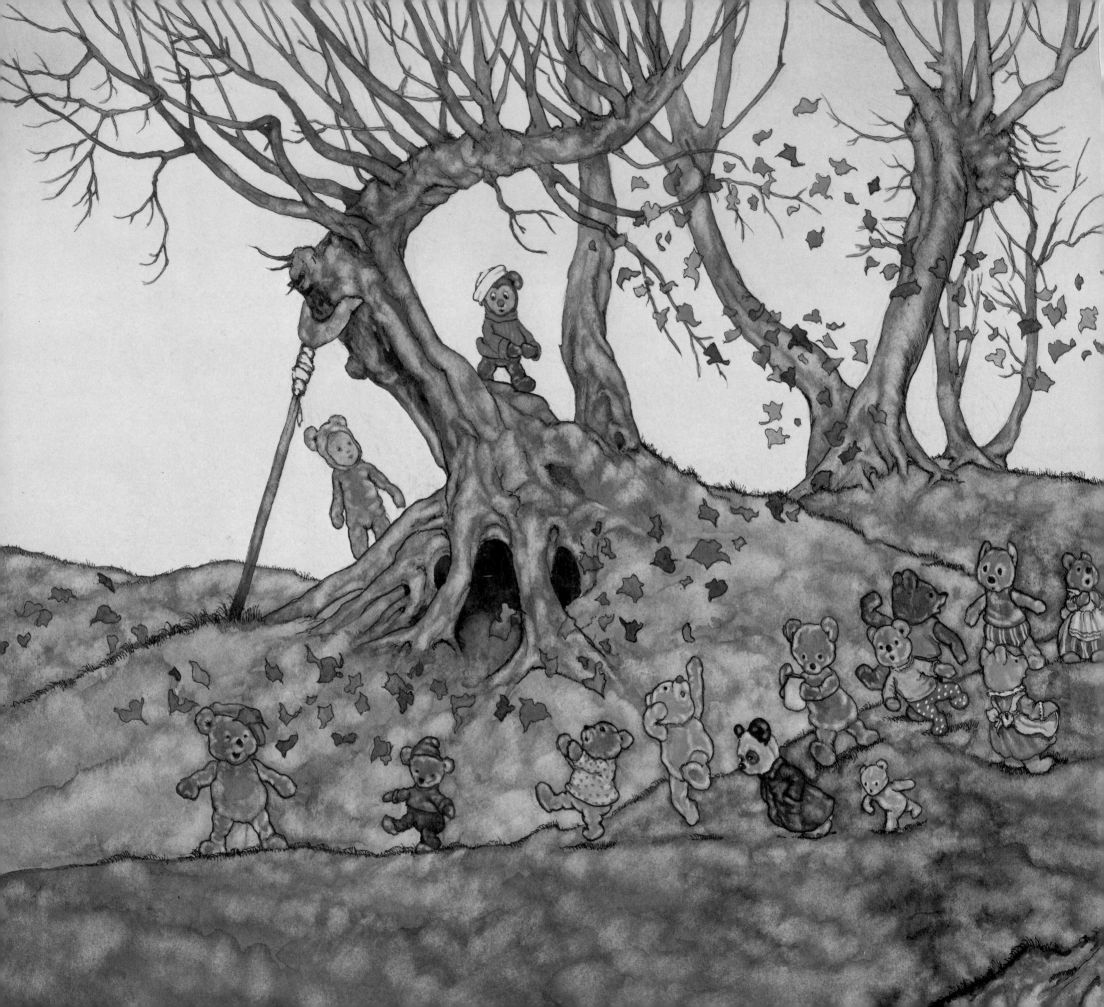

'Cause that's the way the Teddy Bears
Have their picnic.

If you go down in the woods today
You'd better not go alone.

It's lovely down in the woods today
But safer to stay at home.

For ev'ry Bear that ever there was
Will gather there for certain, because
Today's the day the Teddy Bears have
Their picnic.

Picnic time for Teddy Bears,
The little Teddy Bears are having
A lovely time today.
Watch them, catch them unawares
And see them picnic on their holiday.

See them gaily gad about,
They love to play and shout;
They never have any care;

At six o'clock their Mummies
And Daddies
Will take them home to bed,

Because they're tired little Teddy Bears.

Books Illustrated by Michael Hague

Alphabears
An ABC Book
by Kathleen Hague

Bear Hugs
by Kathleen Hague

Calendarbears
A Book of Months
by Kathleen Hague

A Child's Book of Prayers

Michael Hague's Family
Christmas Treasury

Michael Hague's Favourite
Hans Christian Andersen Fairy Tales

Mother Goose
A Collection of Classic Nursery Rhymes

The Night Before Christmas
by Clement C. Moore

Numbears
A Counting Book
by Kathleen Hague

Old Mother West Wind
by Thornton W. Burgess

Peter Pan
by J. M. Barrie

The Reluctant Dragon
by Kenneth Grahame

The Teddy Bears' Picnic
by Jimmy Kennedy

The Velveteen Rabbit
or How Toys Become Real
by Margery Williams

The Wind in the Willows
by Kenneth Grahame

The Wizard of Oz
by L. Frank Baum